The Big Dark

Imagine a cold winter morning

when you have to leave your snuggly bed

to go out with Mum and Dad or to playschool.

This story is about Chinoo, who lives in a

much, much colder land in the north,

near the Arctic circle.

Winter days are so short here that

it does not get properly

light for weeks on end.

That is why it is called the *Big Dark*.

The Big Dark

JOHN PRATER

RED FOX

In a distant, dark, cold
land lived little Chinoo
with his parents,
in a house
built of
snow.

It was winter and Chinoo was fed up.

The big cold had frozen the sea solid,
so he couldn't go fishing.

The big wind blew nearly every day,
so he couldn't play outside.

And the Big Dark was everywhere – all the time.

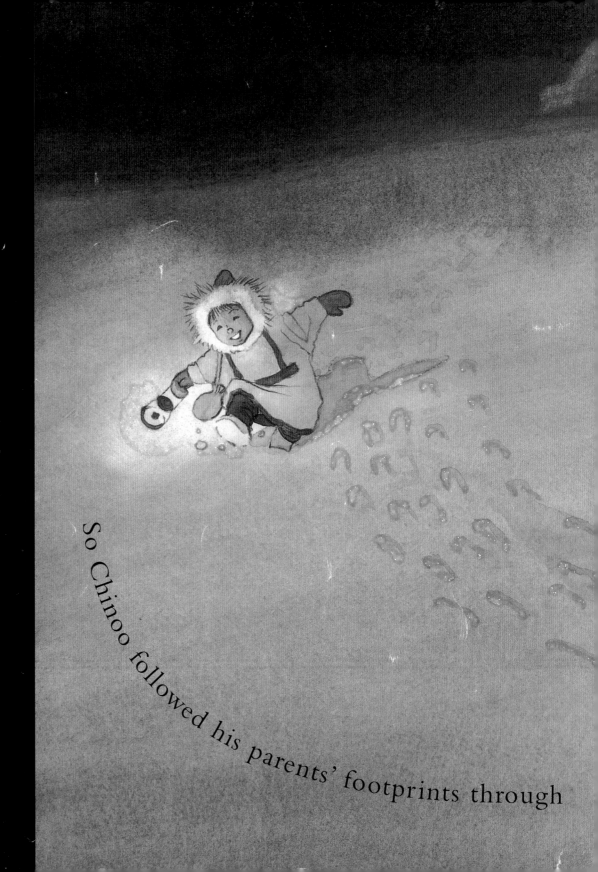

One morning,
when Chinoo looked
outside into the Big Dark,
all was quiet and still.

"Come, little Chinoo,"
said Mama and Papa,
"it's time to go."
"Where?" asked Chinoo.
"To the sea," they said.

So Chinoo followed his parents' footprints through

the snow.

Soon he saw some

BIG,

wide

tracks.

Chinoo scampered
after them
and found . . .

. . . a young polar bear heading for the sea.
"Want to play a game?" asked Chinoo.
"Oh yes, please!" said the polar bear.

So they played hide-and-seek. The bear hid, while Chinoo counted to ten.

1
2
3
4
5
6
7
8
9
10

"I'm coming!"

"This is easy," thought Chinoo. "Just follow the tracks!"

"Found you!" giggled Chinoo. "Now it's my go."

But before the bear could start counting, Chinoo heard his parents calling:
"Come, little Chinoo, hurry up or we'll miss it!"

"Miss what?" asked Chinoo.
"You'll see," they replied.

So Chinoo followed
his parents' footprints
through the
snow again.

Soon, he saw a set of small, round prints. He scampered after them and found . . .

A wolf cub heading for the sea.
"Want to play a game?" asked Chinoo.
"Oh yes, please," replied the wolf cub.

Chinoo took a ball out of his bag and threw it as far as he could.

"Yippee!" said the wolf cub, who scampered after it . . .

. . . and brought it back.

But before Chinoo could throw it again,
he heard his parents calling:

"Come on, Chinoo, hurry or we will miss it!"

"Miss what?" asked Chinoo.
"You'll see," they replied.

Once again, Chinoo plodded on, following
his parents' footprints through the snow.

Soon, he saw
a set of enormous,
wide tracks. He
scampered after
them and found . . .

. . . a young walrus and a daddy walrus,
gallumphing through the snow.

"Want to play a game?"
asked Chinoo.
"What?" puffed the daddy
walrus. "No, no, no, no, no.
We're going to the sea and
we're very late!"

Chinoo's legs suddenly
felt really tired. "It's such
a long way to the sea,"
he said. "I'm tired of
walking and I want to play!"

"How about a lift?" offered the daddy walrus.
"Oh, thank you!" said Chinoo. Quickly, he climbed on board.

It was the wobbliest ride ever,
like sitting on a giant jelly. Soon, they
caught up with Mama and Papa, and
together they walked on through the Big Dark.

Chinoo was amazed to see so many tracks in the snow, all heading in the same direction. At last, as they rounded a corner, they saw the frozen sea.

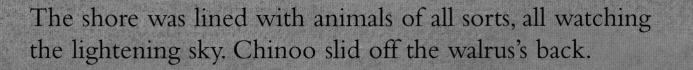

The shore was lined with animals of all sorts, all watching
the lightening sky. Chinoo slid off the walrus's back.

"What's happening?" he asked.
"Shhh," said Mama,
"just watch and wait . . ."

Chinoo watched

and waited,

and waited

and watched,

and then,

very,

very slowly,

it happened.

"Oooooh . . .
Look!" said Chinoo.
"Mmmmmm!"
said the animals.

"The sun!"

"At last!" whispered Mama. "The Big Dark is over.
The sun will shine and the ice will melt."
"We can go fishing again and play outside any time," said Papa.

"Yippee!" cried Chinoo.

He skipped all the way home
and he didn't feel tired at all!

For Ellie and Adam

THE BIG DARK
A RED FOX BOOK 978 0 099 48752 4

First published in Great Britain by Red Fox,
an imprint of Random House Children's Books
A Random House Group Company

This edition published 2007

1 3 5 7 9 10 8 6 4 2

The Random House Group Limited makes every effort to ensure that the papers used in its books are
made from trees that have been legally sourced from well-managed and credibly certified forests.
Our paper procurement policy can be found at: www.randomhouse.co.uk/paper.htm

Red Fox Books are published by Random House Children's Books,
61-63 Uxbridge Road, London W5 5SA

Addresses for companies within The Random House Group Limited can
be found at: www.randomhouse.co.uk/offices.htm

THE RANDOM HOUSE GROUP Limited Reg. No. 954009

www.**kids**at**randomhouse**.co.uk
www.rbooks.co.uk

A CIP catalogue record for this book is available from the British Library.

Printed and bound in China